Mila

Has Two Beds

Written by
Judith Koppens

Illustrated
by Anouk Nys

Clavis

NEW YORK

Hi! I'm Mila and this
is my dog, Pepper.
I'm getting ready to go
to my mommy's house.
Don't look so sad, Pepper.
I will be back very soon.

Daddy gets a big hug and I pet Pepper on his head. In a few nights I'll be back.

Bye, sweet Daddy.
Bye, Daddy-house.
Bye, silly dog.

It's really nice at Mommy's house, too.
Ginger is waiting for me, and Mommy
has a big smile. It's nice to be back
here again.

Hello, smiling Mommy.
Hello, Mommy-house.
Hello, soft kitty.

I quickly take off my muddy boots. Mommy doesn't like muddy feet in the house. Daddy never says anything about it. Mommy gives me a nice bath and washes my hair. I love taking baths. Daddy has a shower at his house. Showers are fun.

I brush my teeth with my green toothbrush.
It's standing in a cup in Mommy's
bathroom. It's different at Daddy's.
My toothbrush there is red and
it's on the bottom shelf
so I can reach it myself.

This bed is my bedroom at Mommy's. It's different from my room at Daddy's. But that's okay—I have two beautiful bedrooms and two nice beds, all just for me.

Mommy reads me a bedtime story.
Tonight she is reading one about a magic
butterfly. When Mommy reads a story,
I forget everything around me.
It's different at Daddy's.
He makes up silly songs, like:
Tralalala and hopedeehee,
will you come along with
me? Hoopla, hoopla,
take my hand, then
we'll go to dreamland!

Then Mommy gives me a kiss on both my cheeks. One here and one there. Daddy does it differently— he gives me tickling kisses on my nose.

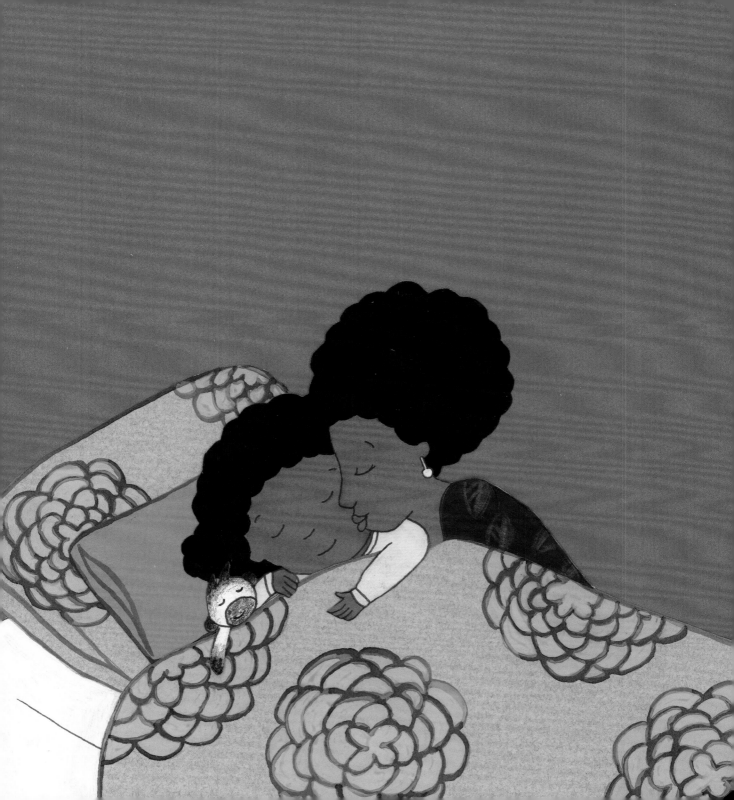

"Good night, my darling," Mommy says.
"Sweet dreams about all nice things."
Daddy says something different:
"Nighty-night, little princess.
I love you very, very much!"

After two nights Mommy brings me back to Daddy. It was nice at Mommy's, but I'm happy to see Daddy again. I get to sit on the back of Mommy's bike. It's different with Daddy—he drives me to Mommy's in his car.

Daddy is waiting for me. "Go to Daddy now," Mommy says softly. She gives me another big hug. "See you soon, darling! Two more nights and then we'll see each other again."

Things are different at Mommy's house than at Daddy's house. But one thing is the same. Mommy and Daddy both love me very much.